GORDON

BARK TO THE FUTURE!

A P.U.R.S.T. ADVENTURE

KIDS CAN PRESS

FOR THE FABULOUS BAKER GIRLS: JULIA, MALIA AND IVORY.

Kids Can Press gratefully acknowledges the financial support of the Government of Ontario, through the Ontario Media Development Corporation; the Ontario Arts Council; the Canada Council for the Arts; and the Government of Canada, through the CBF, for our publishing activity.

Published in Canada and the U.S. by Kids Can Press Ltd.
25 Dockside Drive, Toronto, ON M5A 0B5

Kids Can Press is a Corus Entertainment Inc. company

www.kidscanpress.com

The artwork in this book was rendered digitally in between frequent walks and rounds of BALL!
The text is set in Fontoon.

Edited by Yasemin Uçar
Designed by Julia Naimska

Printed and bound in Shenzhen, China, in 10/2017 by C&C Offset

CM 18 0 9 8 7 6 5 4 3 2 1
CM PA 18 0 9 8 7 6 5 4 3 2 1

Library and Archives Canada Cataloguing in Publication

Spires, Ashley, 1978–, author, illustrator

Gordon : bark to the future! / written and illustrated by Ashley Spires. (A P.U.R.S.T. adventure)

ISBN 978-1-77138-409-4 (hardcover).--ISBN 978-1-77138-410-0 (softcover)

1. Graphic novels. I. Title. II. Series: Spires, Ashley, 1978– . P.U.R.S.T. adventure.

PN6733.S66G67 2018   j741.5'971   C2017-902756-5

NO WORMHOLES
OR TIME VORTEXES
WERE CREATED DURING
THE MAKING OF
THIS BOOK.

IT'S ALL UP TO GORDON NOW.

4

HIS SUPERIOR OFFICER HAS BEEN NEUTRALIZED.

AND GORDON'S DISTRESS CALLS TO P.U.R.S.T. (PETS OF THE UNIVERSE READY FOR SPACE TRAVEL) COMMAND CENTER ...

HAVE GONE UNANSWERED.

THEY DIDN'T SEE IT COMING.

THE ALIENS HATCHED IN THE WALLS.

THEY EMERGED IN THE NIGHT.

AND HIS HUMANS …

BUZZ

AHHHHH!

HIS POOR HELPLESS HUMANS!

THEY GOT THERE AS FAST AS THEY COULD …

BZZZZZ

ARGH!
AHHHHH!

BUT IT WAS TOO LATE.

NOW HE IS A LONE SPACE PET ...

IN THE MIDDLE OF AN ALIEN INVASION.

PHYSICAL COMBAT HAS NEVER BEEN GORDON'S STRENGTH.

BETTER TO LEAVE THE LEAPING AND POUNCING TO THE CATS.

THIS DOG'S DEADLIEST WEAPON IS HIS MIND.

BUT NONE OF HIS COMPUTERS, ROBOTS OR DEVICES
COULD HAVE PREPARED HIM FOR THIS.

THINK, GORDON, THINK!

THERE IS ONLY ONE WAY HE CAN THINK OF ...

TO SAVE HIS FRIENDS ... AND HIS HUMANS.

BUT IT'S TOO DANGEROUS.

NOT NOW, GORDON! FOCUS!

12

THERE IS NO TIME FOR TESTS NOW.

IT'S DANGEROUS, BUT HE DOESN'T HAVE A CHOICE.

THERE IS TOO MUCH AT STAKE.

MMMMM ... STEAK.

zoom

clang

TRAVEL BACK:
5 YEARS

WHIRR

click

rumble

whir

SHAPOW!

HE'S IN HIS SPACE STATION ... BUT THERE ARE NO ALIENS!

THIS CAN ONLY MEAN ONE THING ...

GORDON'S TIME MACHINE WORKED!

NOW HE JUST NEEDS TO STOP THE ALIEN INVASION BEFORE IT STARTS.

BUT HE MUST BE CAREFUL NOT TO CHANGE ANYTHING ELSE.

IF HE CHANGES THE PAST TOO MUCH, HE COULD JEOPARDIZE THE FUTURE, WHICH IS, TECHNICALLY, HIS PRESENT BECAUSE HE'S IN THE PAST.

HOLY HAIR BALLS, THAT'S CONFUSING.

THE PAST SMELLS FUNNY.

SOMETHING IS OFF, BUT HE CAN'T PUT HIS PAW ON IT.

HIS PEE TREE IS SHORTER THAN HE REMEMBERS.

EVEN TED LOOKS DIFFERENT.

IT'S WEIRDLY QUIET, TOO.

ALMOST LIKE SOMETHING IS MISSING ...

HOW COULD THIS HAVE HAPPENED?

HE WENT BACK TOO FAR!

FIVE YEARS TOO FAR!

FIVE YEARS AGO HE WASN'T EVEN BORN YET ...

GRACIE DIDN'T LIVE NEXT DOOR ...

AND BINKY ...

THIS IS BAD.

GORDON WAS BETTER OFF IN THE MIDDLE OF THE ALIEN INVASION.

AT LEAST HE STILL HAS HIS TIME MACHINE.

IN HIS PANIC TO ESCAPE, HE MUST HAVE PUNCHED IN THE WRONG DATE ...

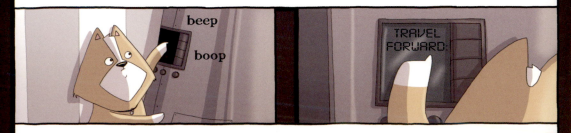

ALL HE HAS TO DO IS ENTER THE TIME HE MEANT TO GO TO AND ...

UH-OH. THAT CAN'T BE GOOD.

NO POWER!

HE IS OUT OF ALLOFUZZIUM!*

*ALLOFUZZIUM IS A SUPER RARE TYPE OF FUEL.
ITS ONLY PURPOSE IS TO MAKE TIME MACHINES WORK.

HIS HUMANS!

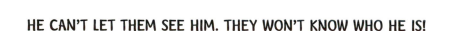

HE CAN'T LET THEM SEE HIM. THEY WON'T KNOW WHO HE IS!

THEY MIGHT THINK HE'S LOST AND CALL ANIMAL CONTROL.

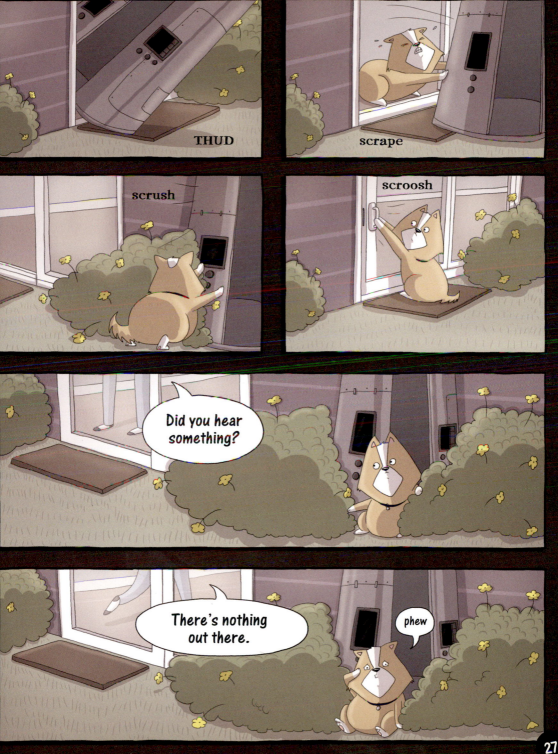

HE HAS TO TRY TO CONTACT P.U.R.S.T. HEADQUARTERS.

SERGEANT FLUFFY VANDERMERE WILL KNOW WHAT TO DO.

HOLY FUTURE FURBALLS! OF COURSE!

P.U.R.S.T. ISN'T P.U.R.S.T.!

IT'S STILL **F.U.R.S.T.** *FELINES* OF THE UNIVERSE READY FOR SPACE TRAVEL!

THEY HAVEN'T STARTED THEIR EQUAL OPPORTUNITY PROGRAM YET,
WHICH MEANS ...

HE WON'T BE GOING ANYWHERE UNLESS HE GETS
SOME MORE ALLOFUZZIUM.

BUT HOW CAN HE FIND SOME WITHOUT P.U.R.S.T. ...

OR HIS LAB ...

OR HIS BONE ...

OR HIS FRIENDS?

WAIT A MINUTE ...
BINKY MIGHT JUST BE A KITTEN AND P.U.R.S.T. MIGHT NOT EXIST ...

BUT CAPTAIN GRACIE IS OUT THERE SOMEWHERE.

IF HE CAN GET HER A MESSAGE ...

GRACIE WILL HELP HIM. HE JUST KNOWS SHE WILL.

ALL HE HAS TO DO IS WAIT.

yawn

IT'S A NEW DAY AND THIS DOG NEEDS A PLAN.

HE MIGHT NOT LIVE HERE YET ...

BUT THIS IS STILL HIS SPACE STATION.

shhoooosh

KITTEN FOOD

crackle

KITTEN FOOD

clunch

KITTEN FOOD

patooo

KITTEN FOOD

munch
crunch

KITTEN FOOD

THERE MUST BE A WAY TO PROTECT THE SPACE STATION **NOW** ...

SO THAT THE ALIENS CAN'T INVADE IN THE FUTURE.

scritch

ALL GOOD SPACE PETS KNOW THAT IF YOU WANT
TO KEEP YOUR SPACE STATION SAFE ...

weak point

weak point

THE FIRST THING YOU HAVE TO DO IS SECURE THE PERIMETER.

BINKY AND GRACIE ALWAYS MADE THIS LOOK SO EASY!

IF HE CAN'T GO UNDER THE SPACE STATION, THEN MAYBE HE CAN GO OVER IT.

HE JUST HAS TO FIGURE OUT A WAY TO GET ON THE ROOF.

THAT'S IT ... HIGHER ...

swish

swoosh

THIS ISN'T WORKING. GORDON IS AN INVENTOR, NOT A LEAPER.

IT'S TIME FOR HIM TO SOLVE THIS THE GORDON WAY ...

BY BUILDING AN ANTI-ALIEN ALARM SYSTEM!

HE DOESN'T HAVE MUCH TO WORK WITH ...

BUT HE'LL MANAGE.

FINISHED! IT WILL LIGHT UP AND SOUND THE ALARM AS SOON AS THIS PART SENSES ANY ALIEN ACTIVITY.

49

Feline Agent Who
Is Not a Dog
292 Sentinal Pkwy

Dear Feline Agent Who Is Not a Dog,

I don't know who you are, but only a true F.U.R.S.T. agent would know how to find me when I'm deep undercover. For that reason, I've had headquarters send you ten millitails of allofuzzium. I hope our paths cross some day.

Good hunting,

Captain Gracie

HE KNEW HE COULD COUNT ON GRACIE.

THIS SHOULD BE JUST ENOUGH FUEL ...

FOR HIM TO STOP THE INVASION AND GET BACK TO THE PRESENT.

THE PRESENT MEANING THE FUTURE ...

GRRR! EITHER WAY, IT'S TIME TO SAVE THE DAY!

ALL RIGHT, BALL, LET'S GO HOME.

RUN! IT'S A SWARM!

COME ON, BINKY!

WHAT IS WRONG WITH YOU? YOU'RE A SPACE PET, NOT A ZOMBIE PET!

BINKY, STOP THEM! THEY ARE TOUCHING TED!

IT'S TED, BINKY!
NO ONE TOUCHES TED.
REMEMBER?!?

SOMETHING IS VERY WRONG.

WHAT COULD HAVE CHANGED BINKY ...

THIS MUCH?

57

HOLY FUZZBUTT!

GORDON CHANGED THE FUTURE!

GORDON STOLE THE KITTEN FOOD THAT HAD THE F.U.R.S.T. FLYER IN IT.

crackle

BAG WITH FLYER IN IT.

KITTEN FOOD

Where did all your food go, Binky?

BAG WITH NO FLYER IN IT.

CAT FOOD LOW FAT LOW CARB LOW FLAVOR

tinkle

SO BINKY NEVER SAW THE FLYER.

AND SINCE HE NEVER SAW THE FLYER ...

HE NEVER BECAME A SPACE CAT!

THE ALIENS HAVE BRAINWASHED HIM TO NOT FIGHT BACK!

GORDON HAS TO FIX THIS.

PROBABLY NOT.

ALSO HE WILL HAVE TO TRAVEL TO THE MOMENT HE LEFT TO
PREVENT A PARADOX, BECAUSE IF HE GETS STUCK IN THE
PAST/FUTURE, THEN THERE WILL BE TWO GORDONS AND
THE UNIVERSE WILL IMPLODE AND ...

DOGGONE IT! HE HAS TO TRY!

IF HE LEAVES THE TIME MACHINE RUNNING ...

HE MIGHT SAVE ENOUGH POWER TO MAKE IT TRAVEL TWICE.

BUT HE WILL ONLY HAVE TWO MINUTES BEFORE IT
AUTOMATICALLY TRAVELS BACK TO HIS TIME.

61

IF GORDON DOESN'T MAKE IT BACK TO THE TIME MACHINE BEFORE IT LEAVES, HE WILL BE STUCK IN THE PAST FOREVER.

BUT WHAT CHOICE DOES HE HAVE? HE HAS TO SAVE THE FUTURE!

WAPOOSH!

crinkle

KITTEN FOOD

munch
crunch

60 SECONDS
TO DEPARTURE

fold

WAIT ...

EVEN IF HE FIXES THIS AND BINKY BECOMES A SPACE CAT AGAIN ...

THAT STILL DOESN'T SOLVE THE ALIEN INVASION!

HE'S ALMOST OUT OF TIME!
BUT THERE IS ONE LAST THING HE CAN TRY!

IT WORKED!

BINKY IS A SPACE CAT AGAIN!

GORDON IS HOME!

BUT WAIT.

GORDON STILL HAS TO STOP THE INVASION!

THERE WON'T BE AN INVASION.

BINKY HAD FIVE YEARS TO PREPARE.

THE ALIENS DIDN'T STAND A CHANCE ...

WITH GORDON TAKING CARE OF THINGS ... FROM THE PAST.

THANKS TO GORDON'S NOTE ...

HIS HUMANS, HIS FRIENDS AND HIS SPACE STATION ARE ALL SAFE.

THIS CALLS FOR A SNACK.

SORRY, ALIEN.

TIME'S UP.